WALT DISNEY PRODUCTIONS
presents

Cinderella's Busy Birthday

Random House 🏠 **New York**

First American Edition. Copyright © 1985 by Walt Disney Productions. All rights reserved under International and Pan-American Copyright Conventions. Published in the United States by Random House, Inc., New York, and simultaneously in Canada by Random House of Canada Limited, Toronto. Originally published in Denmark as DYRENE HJAELPER ASKEPOT by Gutenberghus Gruppen, Copenhagen. ISBN: 0-394-87585-0 Manufactured in the United States of America 9 0 B C D E F G H I J K

Book Club Edition

Cinderella was a sweet and pretty girl.
She lived with her mean stepmother and
her stepsisters, Drizella and Anastasia.
They made Cinderella work very hard.

"It will be my birthday in a few days,"
Cinderella said to her stepmother one day.
"May I have that day off for a picnic?"

"Only if all your chores are done,"
said the stepmother.

Cinderella was kept busy
from sunrise to sunset.

She lit the fire
in the early morning.

She mended her
stepsisters' dresses
in the evening.

Cinderella's only friends
were the birds and the mice.
They liked to visit her
in her attic room.

Cinderella always gave the birds
bread crumbs to eat.

She fed the mice cookies
that were left over.

Cinderella even saved scraps of cloth
from her mending.
She used the cloth to sew clothes
for the mice.

"This shirt will keep you warm," Cinderella said to one of the mice, named Gus.

Soon it was the day before
Cinderella's birthday.
"Remember to finish
all of your chores,"
said her stepmother.

Cinderella sang gaily
as she hung up the wash.
  "What a wonderful day
I'll have tomorrow!"
she said to a bird.

  But Cinderella's
stepsisters were
busy plotting.
  "Mother will never
let her have tomorrow
off," said Drizella.
  "Neither will we!"
said Anastasia.

Cinderella woke up bright and early
the next morning.

"What a wonderful day for a picnic!"
she said happily.

"Happy birthday, Cinderella!"
squeaked the mice.

Cinderella looked in the mirror.
"I feel so happy today!" she said.

"I will wear
my best dress
for the picnic,"
Cinderella said.
"Now I must pack
a lunch basket!"

Cinderella hurried downstairs
to the parlor.

"Just a minute, Cinderella!"
said Drizella.

"Some things must be done before you go out," said Anastasia.

Lucifer the cat growled at Cinderella.

He did not like anyone who was friendly with mice!

"This silver
teapot needs
polishing,"
Drizella said.

"And make sure
the chandelier
is dusted,"
said Cinderella's
stepmother.

Then Lucifer meowed
hungrily.
So Cinderella fed him.

Finally Cinderella had done the chores.
She quickly packed a picnic lunch.

"Now I can go
on my picnic!"
Cinderella said.

Cinderella
opened the door
and then—

"My dress!" shouted Drizella.
"My shoes!" called Anastasia.

Cinderella sighed sadly.
She polished Anastasia's shoes.
Lucifer watched Cinderella work.

Then Cinderella
ironed Drizella's
dress.
She worked
as quickly as
she could.

"Finally done!"
said Cinderella.
"Surely there are
no more chores!"
She took off
her apron.

She picked up
her basket and
opened the door.
Then she heard
Drizella's voice.

"Wait a minute!"
called Drizella.

"Before you go, gather all the wood
you see. Stack it in the woodshed. We
will need to keep the stove lit today
while you are gone," Drizella said.

So Cinderella collected sticks of wood.
She did not even complain.
One by one, her friends came by.
"We will help you!" they said to her.

The little birds
picked up small twigs
in their beaks.

The friendly rabbits
hopped up with sticks
held in their mouths
and paws.

"Now it is
our turn to help
Cinderella!"
twittered one
of the birds.

Meanwhile, the stepmother was sitting
at home with Drizella and Anastasia.
"Gathering wood will keep Cinderella
busy for a while," said the stepmother.
"And we can think of some more chores
for her to do!" said Anastasia.

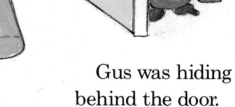

Gus was hiding
behind the door.

"Oh, no! We must
help Cinderella, or
she will never have
her picnic!" he said.
And off he ran
to the kitchen.

Gus told the other mice what he
had heard.

"I have a plan," Gus said to them.
He pointed to the cellar trap door.

"Come with me," Gus said to his pal Jack.
"We'll go down to the cellar. The rest
of you, hide here in the kitchen."

Gus and Jack ran down the steps.
"What should we do?" asked Jack.
"Make a lot of noise!" said Gus.

The mice
banged spoons
together—
CLANG!

They rolled
milk bottles
around—CLINK!

Then Gus
and Jack ran
up the stairs
to the kitchen,
squeaking loudly.

Meanwhile, Cinderella's stepmother and stepsisters had gone into the parlor.

"What else needs to be cleaned here?" asked the stepmother.

"These plates need washing," said Drizella.

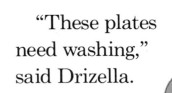

"This chair needs dusting," said Anastasia.

"There's clearly no time for Cinderella to have the day off," said the stepmother.

Then the mean ladies and Lucifer
heard noises from the kitchen.
Clang! Clink! Squeak!
"What's that?" asked Drizella.

They ran into the kitchen.

"It must be those awful mice, down
in the cellar again!" said the stepmother.
"We can get rid of them, now that Cinderella
is out of the house. Come, girls—and you
too, Lucifer!"

The stepmother tiptoed down the stairs.
Drizella and Anastasia followed her.
"It's so dusty!" said Drizella.
"And dark!" said Anastasia.
"Don't be a scaredy-cat, Lucifer.
Find those mice!" said the stepmother.

"Okay, everyone!" Gus said to the mice
in the kitchen. "Let's get to work!"

The mice pushed
against the trap door
as hard as they could.

It snapped shut!

"Hooray! We
did it!" cheered
the mice. "Now
they will have
to find their
way upstairs
in the dark—
and that will
take some time!"

By this time, Cinderella had gathered
all the sticks of wood.

"Now it must
be time for my
picnic. There is
still half a day
left," she said.

There was no one
around to give Cinderella
another chore to do.
So she skipped off
to have her picnic
with all her friends.

"Wait for us!"
squeaked the mice.

Cinderella found a lovely spot
for her picnic.

The woodland animals, the birds,
and the mice gathered around her.

"This has been a busy, busy birthday,"
Cinderella said. "I am glad that you are
here to celebrate it with me."

The animals were glad too.

They had helped Cinderella to have
her picnic—and that was the best present
they could give her!